DEDICATION

To all our aunts & uncles, who visit us every Christmas. We love celebrating with you.

THIS BOOK BELONGS TO:

_____

_____

The Unicorn Farm family loves celebrating the holidays together.

Before the holiday season starts, they have fun together decorating for Christmas, sleeping in, and drinking hot chocolate.

In the wintertime, Holland loves snow, wearing winter hats and scarves in the cold, and learning how to ice skate.

Ryder is turning four this year. As he gets older, he wants to spend more and more time with his big sister. One of the things Holland and Ryder like to do together in the wintertime is pretend to have snowball fights.

Holland's favorite thing about the holidays is spending time with her family, especially when aunts and uncles come to the farm to visit.

They love to watch Christmas movies, eat lots of food, and bake desserts.

She also loves gathering around the tree and handing out presents!

Holland loves to bake gingerbread cookies with Aunt Amber. Aunt Amber is the best baker in the family. This is a new tradition in their family, and it's an especially delicious one!

Traditions are an important part of celebrating the holidays for the Unicorn Family.

The Unicorn Family is a blended family. That means they have traditions from their mom, dad, step-mom, and step-dad.

It also means they get to make up new traditions with their new family! Making gingerbread cookies with Aunt Amber is one of those new traditions.

Brooke brought them the tradition of making reindeer food on Christmas Eve.

Mom brought them the tradition of opening one present together on Christmas Eve.

Happy christmas

Max brought them the tradition of making homemade caramels.

Dad brought them the tradition of wearing matching pjs every year.

Celebrating traditions is so fun and they help the family bond even more closely together.

About the Authors

Bianca Munce is a licensed professional counselor in Virginia. A native New Yorker, Bianca loves her life with her husband Bryan, their three dogs, and four kiddos. Bianca co-authored the Unicorn Farm Series with her youngest step-daughter Hannah.

Hannah-Joie is a ten-year-old fifth grade student. She is a competitive dancer and a lover of animals. Hannah has six pets, three cats and three dogs. She also has two sisters and two brothers! She loves to spend time with her family, watch movies, and wear anything pink. This is the third book Hannah has written in the Unicorn Farm Series. When she grows up, she'd love to be a dancer on Broadway, a teacher, a veterinarian, and continue to be an author.

Made in United States
Orlando, FL
27 November 2024

54583079R00027